FRieNds

& The DisTaNce BeTweeN

WRiTTeN & iLLUsTRATed
By duG NAP

i'M NOT SuRe why, buT
everyONe seemed TO Keep THeiR
distANCe FROM BOb KLiNK.

4

even
Bob's
cat,
Snooper,
seemed
to
stay
back.

MeOW
MeOW
MeOW*
*TRANSLATION: i'd RATHER be by MYSELF, Bob.

There was
also a great
distance between Bob
and the guy who lived in
Bob's bathroom.

Hey, Bob- can you come in the bathroom for a minute so we can talk?
Sorry- i gotta go outside now, then i'm going to Cowboy Steve's.

A LOT OF PEOPLE THOUGHT BOB should GET TO KNOW his NEIGHBOR, COWBOY STEVE, BUT BOB THOUGHT COWBOY STEVE TALKED TOO MUCH ABOUT himSELF.

WHAT AM i - his THeRAPisT?
Guess WHAT, Bob? i SAW MY ex-GiRLFriend KiSSiNG SOME GuY iN THe MALL. iT MADE Me FeeL KiNDA' WeiRD, Bob. NOT AT FiRST, buT THeN iT did. KNOW WHAT i MEAN?

And Bob thought
Cowboy Steve
asked too many
Personal questions.

So, why don't you use your bathroom, Bob?
Well, cowboy— it's a pretty long story.

ALThough he didN'T haVe ANy
FRieNds, Bob did SORT OF KNOW
WiLLy The WORM - A KiNd OF
FAMOUS dRUMMER who used TO
eMAiL Bob his UPCOMING
TOUR daTes FOLLOwed by
A CORNy joKe.

BOB,
bosTon 9/1
New York 9/2
PhiLLy 9/3
bALTimore 9/4
wash. dc 9/6
RichmonD VA 9/8
Hope 2 c u THeRe
PS - Why did The GoLFer bRinG Two PaiRs of PanTs?*
*in Case he GoT A hoLe-in-one

14

He ALSO KNeW AN ACTOR NAMed
BRiAN RyAN O'BRieN The III
whO ONLy CALLed wheN he WAS
MANY sheeTS TO The wiNd.

"Hey, Killer -
how's my bro' doin'?
i'm just about to do
some more blow so i thought i'd
call you, (SNORT)
Man, This
blow is
so
intense,
Bob."

There, too, was a woman
named Jessica Jane who would
leave messages for Bob.
Unfortunately, he couldn't
trust her to tell the truth.

Bob, hey,
i just wanted to
let you know
that just because
i don't call you
doesn't mean
i don't think
about you
all the
time!
OGM1
OGM2
Answer
Delete
Play
Repeat
Skip
Time Set

BUT BOB COULdN'T heLP buT
THINK THAT Jessica JANe WAS
LeAdING hiM ON.

WHAT DO YOU MEAN THAT I'VE BEEN BREAD CRUMBING* YOU, BOB?
YOU KEEP SAYING WE'LL GO OUT, BUT WE NEVER DO!
*BREADCRUMBING: FLIRTING TO KEEP SOMEONE INTERESTED.

20

There was also Julianne Winnetka, who sometimes would take Bob to the supermarket. He'd shop while she waited in her car. Since she was so nice - he offered to buy her lunch.

NO, i COULdN'T HaVe LUNch WiTh yOu
becaUse PeOPLe MiGhT see us & GeT
The idea ThaT we'Re seeinG eacH oTheR.

Bob thought his insurance agent, John Turnscrew, was funny, so he asked him if he'd like to have coffee.

24

THeN, BOb exchANGed a
FLURRy OF eMAiLs WiTh MARy
"WhiTe-bReAd" WiLLiams. BUT
wheNeVeR he cALLed heR, she
WOULdN'T PicK UP The PHONe.
She WOULd WRiTe, Tho'.

Hi Bob

i just wanted
to tell you
that i like
emailing you,
but i don't
want to talk
on the phone
with you!

Bye for now
Mary

Bob had an idea: Maybe his other neighbor would like to go to a movie. So Bob knocked on apartment #5; however, Rudy Pearls, who hailed from New Haven, Connecticut & loved wallpaper said...

i CAN'T COME TO THE door. i'M SURFiNG
THE WEB & i'M COMPLeTeLY NAKed, Bob.

Then there was Abby A.B.
Burns, who loved talking on
the phone with Bob.
But she'd never initiate
calls, and that was
important to him.

yes, i LiKE TALKiNG WiTH you, iT's FUN,
buT NOT so FUN THAT i'd ACTUALLY
CALL you, buT iF you'd LiKE TO
CONTiNUE TO CALL me, WeLL, i GUESS
you CAN, buT i'd NEVER CALL you.

One day Bob met a guy named
edward Dickman, who only
liked to be called
eddie. They seemed to have a
lot in common.

Yeah, i like Leonard Cohen and i also like Cowboy Junkies!
You too, huh? Yeah, sad music is great. Let's hang out!

But did Edward - i mean Eddie - want to be friends? it didn't seem so. it seemed Like Eddie only wanted one thing.

CAN i bORROW
ANOTHER
50 bucks, BOb?
WHAT do you
say? i'LL
PAy you bACK!

iT LooKed PROMiSiNG wheN BoB MeT DobROcheV, A FeLLOw ARTiST (who MAybe SOLd dRuGs ON The side). BuT DobRO WAS ALWAys LATe, ANd ReLiAbiLiTy WAS iMPORTANT TO Bob, so he decided he NO LONGeR WANTed TO hANG OuT WiTh hiM.

& DOBROCHEV SAID, "THE HELL WITH YOU, BOB!" THEN HE STORMED OUT.

AFTeR THAT, THeRe WAS A PoLice WOMAN NAMed Susie Q. CadwaLLadeR. BuT much TO Bob's ANNOYANCe, she OFTeN GAVe him mixed messAGes.

yes, i have a Phone, buT
i don'T answer iT. Give me
A CALL-i'LL buY You Lunch.

Then, Bob contacted Lisa Lovely, who once said to him while they were making love - "Can you imagine how little i like you, Bob?" She was a big time TV Producer down in New York City now, but she answered her phone.

i'M SORRY. i diDN'T MEAN TO ANSWER The Phone. i ThoughT you WERE someone eLse, Bob.

40

One day Bob met Veronika
Monique. She was sooooo nice.
She had a cat too, so Bob
fantasized about the four
of them living together. And
just like he'd hoped, he got a
call from her the very next
day...

i'm sorry, i talked with my fiance and he doesn't want me to have tea with you.

Next, Bob told Charles
Elmtree - an advertising exec.
- that he'd been trying to
find a friend. Charles said he
didn't want to be Bob's friend,
but he gave Bob some advice.

FOLLOW THE PATH TO THE OPEN dOOR.
CREATE NO dRAMA, FAN ALL FLAMES

44

Charles Elmtree also Suggested that Bob go to a bar to meet someone. And he advised him to see a psychiatrist, So Bob went to the Local Lesbian bar.

HeLLO THeRe, LaDies— hOW ARe YOU?
DON'T CALL US LaDies!

THAT CONFUSED BOb.

WeLL, WHAT WOULD YOU LiKE TO be CALLed?
HOW AbOUT YOU DON'T CALL US ANYTHING, MISTER?

THaT aLSO CONFuSeD BOb. SO,
WHeN THey TuRNeD THeiR bACKS
ON BOb, he SPOTTeD A bLONde iN
THe CORNeR AND STARTed
CHaTTiNG heR uP.

...WeLL you seem VeRY Nice, STePhaNeLLa, & i just Love YouR hair.
AND you do, TOO, Bob, but just in CASE you'Re WONDeRING— i'M NOT LOOKiNG FOR A NiCe GUY. NOW iF YOU'LL exCuSe Me, PLeASe.

What did Bob do Next?
Well, Bob had Lunch with
Evelyn Eve Van Dyck who
claimed to be his sister, &
they talked about
friendship. One thing she
said surprised Bob.

i don't think men and women can be friends-could you pass the wine, please?

52

The thing about Juanita
Peterson, was that she was
quite willing to initiate a
phone call. In fact - Juanita
did it ALL the time -
several times a day!

where were you, damn it? you were supposed to
be waiting by the phone like i told you to.

AFTER JUANITA, BOB decided
TO visiT his sTeP MOTHER, ROSE
KLINK. He WAS hoPeFuL TiMe
hAd heALed ALL wouNds.

WHAT do you WANT, ROBERT— why ARE you here?
i WANT TO TALK AbOUT FRIENDSHIP, ROSE.

BeiNG THAT Rose didN'T haVe
aNY FRieNds, she WAS
PRobAbLy NOT The besT
PersON TO ask. & he PRobAbLy
shouLdN'T haVe CALLed heR by
her NAMe because his
sTepMOTHeR didN'T LiKe THAT.

NO, ROBERT- DON'T ASK ME ABOUT
FRIENDSHIP. THAT'S WAY TOO PERSONAL.

iT TOOK A WHiLe FOR BOb TO ASK his dad because his sTePMOTHeR KePT VeRY CLOse WATCH OVeR hiM, buT he FiNALLy GOT hiM ALONe. "HAROLd," he SAid, "HOW do i FiNd A FRieNd?"

SIR, DON'T CALL ME HAROLD - I'M YOUR DAD. AND A MAN DOESN'T NEED A FRIEND . ALL WE NEED IS A NICE CAR, A GOOD LAWN MOWER, AND A WIFE WHO'S WILLING TO GO OUTSIDE AND CHECK FOR SNAKES!

SO BOb decided TO GO see A PSYCHIATRIST.

i CAN heLP you, Bob. By The Time We FiNish you'LL have AT LeasT Ten FRiends.

The PSYCHIATRIST WAS
heLPFuL. They TALKed AbOuT
BOb's STepMOTheR & The Guy
who Lived iN BOb's bAThROOM &
his SHRiNK SuggeSTed THAT BOb
TALK WiTh hiM eveN Though BOb
didN'T LiKe This Guy.

BUT BOB WAS AFRAID

FOR A LONG TIME, BOB JUST
SAT PUT. THEN, HE decided TO
START A CLUB FOR RECLUSES.
BUT did ANYONE COME TO
THE FIRST MEETING?

SORRY, Bob, i'M JUST GOING TO
STAY home AGAIN TONITE, TOO.

ONe summer morning, Bob met
a very attractive Lady at
the Farmers Market and he
had a hunch that she would
be a good friend. She seemed
open, and honest, too.
FINALLy - A COMPANION!

Hi, There.
i'm Crow
Withers-
what's New,
Bob?

Well, uh-
i just
bought a
brand new
bed.

AFTeR TALKiNG A WHiLe THey
decided TO GeT TOGeTHeR. BOb
FeLT LUCKy. AT LeAST UNTiL
he PiCKed HeR UP FOR THeiR
dATe. BeCAUSe MAybe SHe WAS
A LiTTLe TOO OPeN, ANd MAybe A
LiTTLe TOO hONeST?

Hey, Bob, i just had
The best Phone sex
i ever had with This
Russian Plumber
Guy. Too Fun!
Hey, DON'T
TeLL me
THAT!
i'M yOUR
daTe!

A FeW MONThs PASSed & BOb
STARTed hANGING OUT WITh A
WOMAN NAMed JeNNiFeR
GoodMAN & They ReALLy hiT iT
OFF. BiG TIMe!

Let's be friends forever, Bob-ok?

They did so much together -
movies, plays, and dinner
- and Bob was so happy.
Unfortunately, forever
only lasted for two weeks.
And then she *ghosted him, and
later she kept **zombie-ing
him.

*ending a relationship without explanation

**when someone who has ghosted you comes back
to haunt you

Hi handsome, just wanted to check in
with you and see how you're doing.

Then one morning Bob found an invitation in his mailbox from Emily Newington Tidbit. She had a home in Vermont, an apartment in London, and also a house in Nantucket. So she wasn't around much. But the rich fascinated Bob.

DeaR BoB-

i'M haViNG A
PARTY This
COMiNG FridaY.
i CAN'T MaKe iT,
buT i hope you
CAN!

Love
em

WheN Bob meT CaNdy Cummings, he was exTRemely aTTRacTed To her. She had bLONde haiR, GReeN eyes, & she was ReaLLy smaRT. i meaN This was iT. TRue Love wiTh a CaPiTaL "T". He kNew RighT away ThaT he had To PoP The QuesTioN.

i'M
ReaLLY
PReTTY
boRiNG
AND i'M
NOT
THaT
GOOd
LOOKiNG
CANdy,
buT
dO
yOU
THiNK
We
COULd
HAVe
COFFee
SOMeTiMe ?

WeLL, she said yes &
BeLieve iT oR NOT, They FeLL
MADLY iN Love & They sTARTed
TO SPeNd ALL TheiR TiMe
TOGeTheR uP AT heR PLAce iN
The couNTRy & Bob FeLT so
GReAT THAT ALL his haiR GRew
bacK. He KNew TheN THAT his
STORy wouLd haVe A haPPy
eNdiNG.

i Love you, Bob. i Love you CANdy, ANd i
Think AbouT you ALL The Time, honey.
i Think AbouT you ALL The Time, Too, bAbe.
ANd i Love sTAyiNG WiTh you, CANdy.

But Candy's dog, Chaka, didn't like Snooper, so Bob had to leave him at home. & Snooper missed going outside to see all his cat pals. Yes, Snooper wanted a friend, too.

MEOW

AFTeR a whiLe, Bob
ReaLized THAT CANdy & he
didN'T haVe much iN COMMON;
he had A TiNy APT, CANdy had A
biG house. He had AN OLd bike,
she had A Mercedes & A New
TRUCK. Bob ThOuGhT TheiR
diffeReNces weRe NOThiNG They
couLdN'T woRK Through...

i KNOW i'M A THERAPIST, BUT i JUST DON'T
WANT TO TALK ABOUT IT WITH YOU, BOB.

For some reason, Bob couldn't help thinking things would be better if he moved in with her.

Wow,
And Candy's
bed is even
bigGer
Than mine.
& iT'LL be
Fun To be
A dAd,
Too.

BuT THAT idea made caNdy
Nervous & THAT made Bob
aNxious which made
CaNdy more Nervous & TheN
CaNdy's Kid - HaKeem - had
someThiNG TO saY...

MOM - you've GOT To GeT rid of This
Bob TurKey. My doG doesN'T LiKe
Bob Guy eiTher! KicK him ouT of bed, MA.

So Bob went back to his
psychiatrist, but he was met
with a big suprise.

i REALiZe i TOLd you THAT you'd haVe TeN
FRiends by The Time We FiNshed TheraPy, buT
MY husbaNd LeFT me, so i'M MOVING baCK To ALAbaMA.

AFTer his psychiatrist abandoned him, Bob started feeling intense anxiety in his chest. The only thing that helped was to exercise & call Candy several times a day. but how did Candy feel?

Bob! STOP CALLING Me!
PLAY
STOP

AFTER 7 days OF CALLING CANdy, BOb STOPPed. TheN he STARTed bOMbARdiNG his PSychiATRIST WiTh CALLs ANd he LeFT MULTiPLe MessAGes FOR heR, beFORe FiNALLy ReAchiNG heR.

Bob,
i CAN'T
TALK
NOW,
buT i
WANT
TO
ACKNOWLeDGe
THAT YOUR
NeeD TO
TALK
WiTH
Me iS
ReALLY
GReAT.

WheN Bob huNG uP, he
LeaRNed THAT someONe he
ReaLLy Liked had RUN AWAY
FROM home.

here, KiTTy, KiTTy, KiTTy.
here, KiTTy, KiTTy, KiTTy.

A Few days LATeR, BOb cALLed
his PSYCHiATRisT bACK.

...bUT CANdy doesN'T Love me, MicheLLe.
This isN'T AbouT CANdy, Bob-iT's AbouT YouR STep-moTHeR!

They ONLy TALKed A ShORT
Time because his PSychiATRIST
WAS LeAViNG FOR ALAbAMA,
buT she CALLed him bACK A
weeK LATeR.

Bob, i sTiLL CAN'T TALK 'CAuse i'm GoinG To see my new TherAPisT, buT you musT sPeAK To The Guy in your bAThroom. iT's reALLy imPorTANT, Bob!

With no one else to turn to,
Bob finally decided to go in
and meet the guy who lived in
his bathroom.
His name was also Bob.

Hi Bob- how are you? Long time no see.
Hi, Alsobob. Actually i'm feeling kind of down.

iT TURNed OUT-
They HAd A LOT iN COMMON.

SO, YOU'RE ALL ALONE, TOO, ALSOBOB?
YEAH, WHEN YOU COME IN HERE- YOU NEVER SEEM TO NOTICE ME!

AFTER THAT,
BOB BEGAN SPENDING
A LOT OF TIME
WITH ALSOBOB.

So you WANTA' MAybe GO OUT TONIGHT, ALsobob?
Sounds GOOd TO Me, BOb. LeT's do iT!

That evening, Bob and
Alsobob took a long walk
through Starksbend Park.

WHAT do you THINK ABOUT THE WOMAN SITTING ON THE bENCH behiNd ME, ALSObob?

FROM WHAT YOU'VE TOLd ME- YOU SEEM LIKE YOU'RE ALWAYS PICKING THE WRONG PERSON, Bob. MAYbe GIVE IT A REST FOR A WHILE?

So Bob gave it a rest.
And then a strange thing
happened.

BOB! YOU'RE STARTING TO GLOW
SO AREN'T YOU, ALSOBOB!

And Bob's glow - if that's
what did it - seemed to make
people he knew act
differently towards him, like
for instance - Cowboy Steve.

Bob - Good To see you. And
LeT's noT TALK abouT me.
LeT's TALK abouT you!
How have you been, Bob?

& iT seemed TO hAVe AN
AFFecT ON Abby A.B. BuRNs,
As weLL. BecAuse AFTeR he
bumPed iNTO heR ON The sTReeT,
she cALLed him.

Hi Bob - Yeah, it's me again
Can you believe it?
i'm actually initiating
a phone call.

IN FACT, BOB's GLOW seemed
TO AFFeCT A LOT OF PeOPLe he
KNew.

Hi, There Bob. You up for a little golf next week?
Yo, Bobby! i've got that 50 bucks i owe you. Stop by huh?.
Hey, Bob- lookin' good, guy. Sorry i was always so late. Let's get together and start over, ok man?

even julianne winnetka
became friendlier than she
had been before.

OmG,
Bob - hi!
so Good
To see
you.
You're
Looking
ReaLLy
ReaLLy
Good.

But would Julianne
Winnetka go out to lunch
with him?
Would she be a friend?

NO, i couldN'T have LuNch with you, buT LeT'S STiLL be FRieNds, OK?
WeLL, i couLdN'T CALL You A FRieNd, buT i couLd CALL You A *FRieNd-ie!
*A "FRieNd-ie" is someone who NeveR ACTuALLy sPends Time wiTH you, buT is ALWAys veRy FRieNdLy.

120

iT WAS NiCe TO hAVe LOTS OF
FRieNd-ies. He eVeN GOT
GOOd NeWS FROM his
heAd FRieNd-ie.

Hi, Bob. i'M ON MY WAY bACK FROM ALAbAMA. i'M GeTTiNG bACK WiTh my husband. LeT's TALK soon AND We'LL TRy AND schedule AN APPoiNTMeNT.

iT WAS GReAT TO haVe his PSYCHiATRiST bacK. &
SOMeONe eLSe ReAPPeAReD.

MEOW

ANd whAT abouT CANdy?
Did she AT LeAST become
A FRieNd-ie? NO, BOb NeVeR SAW
CANdy AGAiN.

So, CANDY GoT MARRied, huh?
yEAH, THAT's WHAT i heARd, Bob.

AND eVeN THOUGH JESSICA
JANe GHOSTed BOB TO GO
bACK TO heR husbANd, she
CONTiNUed TO ZOMbie him
eVeRy FeW MONThs.

Hi- Jessica Jane here- just called to check in on you- what's new, handsome?

128

He did RUN INTO his
STePMOTHeR ON The STReeT
once. AND he WAS STiLL
hopeFuL Their dARK PAST WAS
behind THeM.

Hey, Rose - Where ya' going, Mom?
i'm not your MOTHER! & don't CALL me Rose!

130

So i guess the big question is:
Did Bob ever find a you-know-
what? Well, not right off, but
yes, Bob did. In fact, he found
a very good one.

THANKS SO MUCH FOR FRIENDING ME, BOB.
SURE, ALSOBOB. MY PLEASURE.

AND THEN IT WAS TIME TO GET SOME SLEEP.

GOOD NIGHT ALSOBOB. i LOVE you.
i LOVE You TOO, BOb.
See you iN YOUR dREAMS!

The eNd